For

*Special thanks to Sally Nachamkin
for production, casting, styling, and wrangling.
And a thanks to the photography crew:
Norman Smith, assisting;
Biata Smoler, assistant stylist/wrangler;
Carolina Machuca, the Christmas Tree.*

Text copyright © 1998
Peter Pauper Press, Inc.
202 Mamaroneck Avenue
White Plains, NY 10601
All rights reserved
ISBN 0-88088-083-X
Printed in China
7 6 5 4 3 2 1

# Introduction

Santa's little helpers embody all the joys of giving and all the good will of the season. Their spirit and good cheer is visible in the twinkle of children's eyes and is revealed in their laughter.

Santa's little helpers remind us that "shared joy is double joy" and that giving of yourself enriches both the giver and the recipient.

May this blessed season give you and your loved ones a year of joy and peace.

V. U.

Have you had
a kindness shown?

Pass it on.

*Henry Burton*

There is no flying

without wings.

*French proverb*

**W**hat you give

you get,

ten times over.

*Yoruba proverb*

**C**hildren are living
jewels dropped
unsustained from
heaven.

*Robert Pollok*

Divide an orange . . .
it tastes just as good.

*Chinese proverb*

In choosing presents
people should
remember that the
whole point of
a present is that
it is an extra.

*E.V. Lucas*

Raise your sail
one foot and you get
ten feet of wind.

*Chinese proverb*

**S**hall we make a
new rule of life
from tonight:
always to try to
be a little kinder
than is necessary?

*James M. Barrie*

**S**ince we cannot
always get what we like,
let us like what
we can get.

*Spanish proverb*

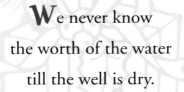

We never know
the worth of the water
till the well is dry.

*French proverb*

When you drink
the water,
remember the spring.

*Chinese proverb*

Kindness is tenderness.
Kindness is love,
but perhaps greater than
love. Kindness is good
will. Kindness says, I
want you to be happy.

*Randolph Ray*

**S**ometimes sharing

your riches is not easy.

*Anonymous*

Sow much, reap much;
sow little, reap little.

*Chinese proverb*

Giving opens the way

for receiving.

*Florence Scovel Shinn*

**I**t is dangerous
to confuse children
with angels.

*David Fyfe*

We must teach
our children to dream
with their eyes open.

*Harry Edwards*

**T**o live in a
blessed world,
share your blessings.

*Anonymous*

Shared joy is
double joy;
shared sorrow is
half a sorrow.

*Swedish proverb*

We can only learn to
love by loving.

*Doris Murdock*

If you are all wrapped
up in yourself
you are overdressed.

*Kate Halvorson*